THE BIG BAD COLD

Adapted by Liz Mills from the
television script "Get Well" by Don Gilles
Illustrated by Carolyn Bracken & Ken Edwards

Based on the Scholastic book series
"Clifford The Big Red Dog"
by Norman Bridwell

ISBN 0-439-38989-5

10 9   08 09

Printed in the U.S.A.
First printing, December 2002

SCHOLASTIC INC.

New York   Toronto   London   Auckland   Sydney
Mexico City   New Delhi   Hong Kong   Buenos Aires

Clifford was waiting for Emily Elizabeth.

T-Bone and Cleo were waiting with him.

They wanted her to come out and play.

Clifford looked in the window.

"Oh, Clifford," Emily Elizabeth said.

"I can't come out today.

I have a bad cold."

"AH-CHOO!"

"What was that?" asked T-Bone.

"Who was that?" asked Cleo.

"It's Emily Elizabeth," said Clifford.

"She's got a bad cold. Poor Emily."

"I know what will make her feel

better," said T-Bone.

"Get-well gifts!"

"We can make her a get-well card!"
Clifford said.

"We can give her a big balloon!" said Cleo.

"We can give her a bunch of flowers!"
T-Bone said.

"And I know just where to find some."

"These flowers are just right, T-Bone,"

said Clifford.

"Uh-oh. Stop, Clifford. Stop!" cried T-Bone.

All the flower tops floated away.

"Sorry," said Clifford.

"That's all right," said T-Bone.

"The flowers look different," Cleo said,

"but they're still pretty."

"Right!" Clifford said.

"Emily Elizabeth will like them."

"We still need a card and a balloon,"

said Cleo.

They walked over to the pier.

"Hey, look at that!" Cleo said.

Samuel was standing in front
of the Fish-and-Chips Shack.
"Free balloons today!" he called.
"Come and get your free balloon!"

Cleo ran to the balloons.

She tried to get one.

She jumped—and the next

thing she knew . . .

. . . she was floating up, up, and away!

Clifford and T-Bone ran after her.

At last, the balloons caught on a flagpole.

Clifford helped Cleo get down.

"How about just one balloon, Cleo?"

said Samuel.

Cleo barked.

"I'll take that as a 'yes,'" Samuel said.

He laughed and tied a yellow balloon

to Cleo's tail.

"I'm glad you're okay, Cleo," said Clifford.

"That's a great balloon!"

Just then, Clifford stepped on

something that was lying on the sidewalk.

"This piece of cardboard would be perfect

for Emily Elizabeth's card," he said.

"But look—I spoiled it!"

"Don't worry, Clifford," said Cleo.

"T-Bone and I will fix it up."

"This is like finger painting, but

I call it body painting!" said T-Bone.

"Looks great!" Cleo said.

"Just one more little spot, right here!"

"Perfect!" said Clifford.

"Emily Elizabeth will love it!"

Suddenly, the wind blew the card

over the fence—

right into the Bleakmans' yard!

"Remember—the Bleakmans said we can't go into their yard," Clifford said.

"Not even one paw."

"Then we'll have to get the card some other way," said Cleo.

"Swing T-Bone one more time, Clifford,"

said Cleo.

"He just has to grab the card in his teeth.

You can do it, T-Bone!"

T-Bone went flying, back and forth.

Luckily, Mr. Bleakman didn't see him.

T-Bone went lower and lower.

"You've got it, T-Bone!" said Cleo.

"Yay, T-Bone!" Clifford cheered.

"You did it!"

At last, the dogs were ready

to give Emily Elizabeth her gifts.

"Are these for me?" Emily Elizabeth asked.

"Thank you all!

I feel better already!

I have the best friends in the world."

Do You Remember?

Circle the right answer.

1. Who gave Emily Elizabeth a bunch of flowers?
   a. Mr. Bleakman
   b. Cleo
   c. T-Bone

2. Clifford's gift to Emily was . . .
   a. a candy bar
   b. a big card
   c. a toy

Which happened first?
Which happened next?
Which happened last?
Write a 1, 2, or 3 in the space after each sentence.

1. Samuel tied a balloon
to Cleo's tail.   _____

2. Emily Elizabeth was in
bed with a cold.   _____

3. The wind blew the card into
the Bleakmans' yard.   _____

Answers:

The wind blew the card into the Bleakmans' yard. (3)
Emily Elizabeth was in bed with a cold. (1)
Samuel tied a balloon to Cleo's tail. (2)
2. b
1. c